T0153431

THE LITTLE BOOK OF
ALICE

Published by OH!
20 Mortimer Street
London W1T 3JW

ISBN 978-1-91161-039-7

Editorial: Victoria Godden, Stella Caldwell
Project manager: Russell Porter
Design: Tony Seddon
Production: Jess Arvidsson

A CIP catalogue for this book is available from the British Library

Printed in Dubai

10 9 8 7 6 5 4 3 2 1

Illustrations: John Tenniel

THE LITTLE BOOK OF
ALICE

WONDERLAND'S WIT & WISDOM

CONTENTS

INTRODUCTION

FROM the indisputable logic of Tweedledum to the nonsensical riddles posed by the Mad Hatter, the witty rejoinders of the Red Queen to the strange wisdom of the Cheshire Cat, there is no denying that Lewis Carroll's most famous works, *Alice's Adventures in Wonderland* and its sequel, *Through the Looking-Glass*, contain some of the most quotable lines ever written in the English language.

While some are instantly recognisable because of the character that utters them ("Off with his head!" comes to mind as a good example), others are remembered for their sheer strangeness ("Why is a raven like a writing-desk?"). What each one cannot help but convey, however, is a celebration of the power of words – to amuse, confuse and, perhaps most importantly, to make us really *think*.

The books' earliest critics were bemused by the popularity they enjoyed among their younger audiences. They were unable, perhaps, to see the sense that was merely masquerading as nonsense.

Even today, 150 years after the books were first published, there is still more to glean from their pages. Indeed, just when you think you understand the utterly bizarre world of Wonderland, you fall down the rabbit hole once again and realise there is always something new to be found within its colourful and curious depths – whether it's an undiscovered pearl of wisdom, a nugget of simple truth or the perfect put-down.

In the pages that follow you'll find the very best of these under one roof, showcasing not only the most recognisable *bon mots* of Wonderland, but the hidden depths and deeper meanings to be found within even the most innocuous turns of phrase…

....

CHAPTER
ONE

RIDDLES &
REJOINDERS

——◆◆◆——

The many inhabitants of
Wonderland will do nothing if not
keep you on your toes, whether
that be with their seemingly
unfathomable riddles or a simple
yet utterly devastating comeback.
All told, when it comes to
holding your own in a tête-à-tête,
Wonderland is not for the
faint of heart…

🐉

"But I don't want to go among mad people," Alice remarked.

"Oh, you can't help that," said the Cat: "we're all mad here. I'm mad. You're mad."

"How do you know I'm mad?" said Alice.

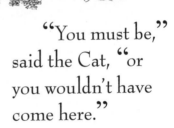

"You must be," said the Cat, "or you wouldn't have come here."

Alice and the Cheshire Cat,
Alice's Adventures in Wonderland

"I don't think—"

"Then you shouldn't talk."

Alice and the Hatter,
Alice's Adventures in Wonderland

"What's the French for fiddle-de-dee?"

"Fiddle-de-dee's not English," Alice replied gravely.

"Who ever said it was?" said the Red Queen.

Alice and the Red Queen,
Through the Looking-Glass

The Hatter's Tea Party

"Then you should say what you mean," the March Hare went on.

"I do," Alice hastily replied; "at least—at least I mean what I say—that's the same thing, you know."

"Not the same thing a bit!" said the Hatter. "You might just as well say that 'I see what I eat' is the same thing as 'I eat what I see'!"

The Hatter's Tea Party,
Alice's Adventures in Wonderland

"I don't like the look of it at all," said the King: "however, it may kiss my hand, if it likes."

The King,
Alice's Adventures in Wonderland

Alice sighed wearily. "I think you might do something better with the time," she said, "than waste it in asking riddles that have no answers."

"If you knew Time as well as I do," said the Hatter, "you wouldn't talk about wasting *it*. It's *him*."

Alice and the Hatter,
Alice's Adventures in Wonderland

"So here's a question for you. How old did you say you were?"

Alice made a short calculation, and said, "Seven years and six months."

"Wrong!" Humpty Dumpty exclaimed triumphantly. "You never said a word like it!"

"I thought you meant 'How old are you?'" Alice explained.

"If I'd meant that, I'd have said it," said Humpty Dumpty.

Alice and Humpty Dumpty,
Through the Looking-Glass

"Would you tell me, please, which way I ought to go from here?"

"That depends a good deal on where you want to get to," said the Cat.

"I don't much care where—" said Alice.

"Then it doesn't matter which way you go," said the Cat.

"—so long as I get somewhere," Alice added as an explanation.

"Oh, you're sure to do that," said the Cat, "if you only walk long enough."

Alice and the Cheshire Cat,
Alice's Adventures in Wonderland

"Have you guessed the riddle yet?" the Hatter said, turning to Alice again.

"No, I give it up," Alice replied: "what's the answer?"

"I haven't the slightest idea," said the Hatter.

Alice and the Hatter,
Alice's Adventures in Wonderland

"And you do Addition?" the White Queen asked. "What's one and one and one and one and one and one and one and one and one and one?"

"I don't know," said Alice. "I lost count."

"She can't do Addition," the Red Queen interrupted.

Alice and the Queens,
Through the Looking-Glass

"Take some more tea," the March Hare said to Alice, very earnestly.

"I've had nothing yet," Alice replied in an offended tone: "so I can't take more."

"You mean you can't take less," said the Hatter: "It's very easy to take more than nothing."

The Hatter's Tea Party,
Alice's Adventures in Wonderland

"Take a bone from a dog: what remains?"

Alice considered. "The bone wouldn't remain, of course, if I took it—and the dog wouldn't remain; it would come to bite me—and I'm sure I shouldn't remain!"

"Then you think nothing would remain?" said the Red Queen.

"I think that's the answer."

"Wrong, as usual," said the Red Queen: "the dog's temper would remain."

Alice and the Red Queen,
Through the Looking-Glass

"Why is a raven like a writing-desk?"

The Hatter,
Alice's Adventures in Wonderland

"O Tiger-lily," said Alice, addressing herself to one that was waving gracefully about in the wind, "I wish you could talk!"

"We can talk," said the Tiger-lily: "when there's anybody worth talking to."

Alice and the Tiger-lily,
Through the Looking-Glass

—∞—

"Take off your hat," the King said to the Hatter.

"It isn't mine," said the Hatter.

"*Stolen!*" the King exclaimed, turning to the jury, who instantly made a memorandum of the fact.

"I keep them to sell," the Hatter added as an explanation: "I've none of my own. I'm a hatter."

The King and the Hatter,
Alice's Adventures in Wonderland

"In most gardens," the Tiger-lily said, "they make the beds too soft—so that the flowers are always asleep."

This sounded a very good reason, and Alice was quite pleased to know it. "I never thought of that before!" she said.

"It's my opinion that you never think at all," the Rose said in a rather severe tone.

Alice and the Flowers,
Through the Looking-Glass

"Your hair wants cutting," said the Hatter. He had been looking at Alice for some time with great curiosity, and this was his first speech.

The Hatter,
Alice's Adventures in Wonderland

"Fan her head!" the Red Queen anxiously interrupted. "She'll be feverish after so much thinking."

The Red Queen,
Through the Looking-Glass

"If that's all you know about it, you may stand down," continued the King.

"I can't go no lower," said the Hatter: "I'm on the floor, as it is."

The King and the Hatter,
Alice's Adventures in Wonderland

"Give your evidence,"
said the King.

"Shan't," said the cook.

The King and the cook,
Alice's Adventures in Wonderland

"Am I addressing the White Queen?"

"Well, yes, if you call that a-dressing," the Queen said. "It isn't my notion of the thing, at all."

Alice and the White Queen,
Through the Looking-Glass

"Please, would you tell me," said Alice, a little timidly, for she was not quite sure whether it was good manners for her to speak first, "why your cat grins like that?" . . .

. . . continued overpage

"**I**t's a
Cheshire
cat," said the
Duchess,
"and that's
why."

Alice and the Duchess,
*Alice's Adventures in
Wonderland*

The Duchess

—∞—

"Rule Forty-two. All persons more than a mile high to leave the court."

Everybody looked at Alice.

"I'm not a mile high," said Alice.

"You are," said the King.

"Nearly two miles high," added the Queen.

"Well, I shan't go, at any rate," said Alice; "besides, that's not a regular rule: you invented it just now."

"It's the oldest rule in the book," said the King.

"Then it ought to be Number One," said Alice.

Alice and the King,
Alice's Adventures in Wonderland

Alice

"I'm a poor man, your Majesty," he began.

"You're a very poor speaker," said the King.

The Hatter and the King,
Alice's Adventures in Wonderland

CHAPTER

TWO

LIFE'S GREAT QUESTIONS & ANSWERS

As a rule, there is always more
to Wonderland than meets the
eye, and even the most innocuous
of questions can reveal a much
greater — in some instances even
philosophical — truth.

And rarely is a "simple" statement
ever as simple as all that…

"Dear, dear! How queer everything is to-day! And yesterday things went on just as usual. I wonder if I've been changed in the night? Let me think: was I the same when I got up this morning? . . .

. . . I almost think I can remember feeling a little different. But if I'm not the same, the next question is, Who in the world am I? Ah, that's the great puzzle!"

Alice, *Alice's Adventures in Wonderland*

"Who are you?" said the Caterpillar.

This was not an encouraging opening for a conversation. Alice replied, rather shyly, "I—I hardly know, sir, just at present—at least I know who I was when I got up this morning, but I think I must have been changed several times since then." . . .

. . . *continued overpage*

The Caterpillar

... "What do you mean by that?" said the Caterpillar sternly. "Explain yourself!"

"I can't explain myself, I'm afraid, sir," said Alice, "because I am not myself, you see."

Alice and the Caterpillar,
Alice's Adventures in Wonderland

"I suppose I ought to eat or drink something or other; but the great question is 'What?'"

Alice,
Alice's Adventures in Wonderland

"I never ask advice about growing," Alice said indignantly.

"Too proud?" the other inquired.

Alice felt even more indignant at this suggestion. "I mean," she said, "that one can't help growing older."

Alice and Humpty Dumpty,
Through the Looking-Glass

"Well, now that we have seen each other," said the Unicorn, "if you'll believe in me, I'll believe in you. Is that a bargain?"

"Yes, if you like," said Alice.

Alice and the Unicorn,
Through the Looking-Glass

"Crawling at your feet," said the Gnat (Alice drew her feet back in some alarm), "you may observe a Bread-and-Butterfly. Its wings are thin slices of Bread-and-butter, its body is a crust, and its head is a lump of sugar."

"And what does it live on?"

"Weak tea with cream in it."

A new difficulty came into Alice's head . . .

"Supposing it couldn't find any?" she suggested.

"Then it would die, of course."

"But that must happen very often," Alice remarked thoughtfully.

"It always happens," said the Gnat.

Alice and the Gnat,
Through the Looking-Glass

"What do you call yourself?" the Fawn said at last. Such a soft sweet voice it had!

"I wish I knew!" thought poor Alice. She answered, rather sadly, "Nothing, just now."

Alice and the Fawn,
Through the Looking-Glass

"Oh, how I wish I could shut up like a telescope! I think I could, if only I knew how to begin." For, you see, so many out-of-the-way things had happened lately, that Alice had begun to think that very few things indeed were really impossible.

Alice,
Alice's Adventures in Wonderland

"I could tell you my adventures – beginning from this morning," said Alice a little timidly, "but it's no use going back to yesterday, because I was a different person then."

Alice,
Alice's Adventures in Wonderland

So she sat on, with closed eyes, and half believed herself in Wonderland, though she knew she had but to open them again, and all would change to dull reality...

Alice's Adventures in Wonderland

"How am I to get in?" asked Alice again in a louder tone.

"Are you to get in at all?" said the Footman. "That's the first question, you know."

Alice and the Footman,
Alice's Adventures in Wonderland

The Footmen

"And what is the use of a book," thought Alice, "without pictures or conversations?"

Alice,
Alice's Adventures in Wonderland

She waited for a few minutes to see if she was going to shrink any further: she felt a little nervous about this, "for it might end, you know," said Alice to herself, "in my going out altogether, like a candle. I wonder what I should be like then?"

Alice's Adventures in Wonderland

"**W**here do you come from?" said the Red Queen. "And where are you going? Look up, speak nicely, and don't twiddle your fingers all the time."

The Red Queen,
Through the Looking-Glass

"Why do you sit out here all alone?" said Alice, not wishing to begin an argument.

"Why, because there's nobody with me!" cried Humpty Dumpty.

Alice and Humpty Dumpty,
Through the Looking-Glass

CHAPTER
THREE

THE WIT &
WISDOM OF
WONDERLAND

Wisdom is often hard to come
by in the real world.

In Wonderland, however,
it appears around every corner,
under every toadstool,
often whether it's asked for
or not…

"When you've once said a thing, that fixes it, and you must take the consequences."

The Red Queen,
Through the Looking-Glass

"You shouldn't make jokes," Alice said, "if it makes you so unhappy."

Alice,
Through the Looking-Glass

"**Q**ueens never make bargains."

The Red Queen,
Through the Looking-Glass

"You may look in front of you, and on both sides, if you like," said the Sheep: "but you can't look all round you—unless you've got eyes at the back of your head."

The Sheep,
Through the Looking-Glass

The Dodo

"Why," said the Dodo, "the best way to explain it is to do it."

The Dodo,
Alice's Adventures in Wonderland

Tweedledee and Tweedledum

"Contrariwise," continued Tweedledee, "if it was so, it might be; and if it were so, it would be; but as it isn't, it ain't. That's logic."

Tweedledee,
Alice's Adventures in Wonderland

"**I**f there's no meaning in it," said the King, "that saves a world of trouble, you know, as we needn't try to find any."

The King,
Alice's Adventures in Wonderland

"Begin at the beginning," the King said gravely, "and go on till you come to the end: then stop."

The King,
Alice's Adventures in Wonderland

"If everybody minded their own business," said the Duchess in a hoarse growl, "the world would go around a great deal faster than it does."

The Duchess,
Alice's Adventures in Wonderland

"Tut, tut, child!" said the Duchess. "Everything's got a moral, if only you can find it."

The Duchess,
Alice's Adventures in Wonderland

The Duchess

"I quite agree with you," said the Duchess, "and the moral of that is—'Be what you would seem to be'—or, if you'd like it put more simply—'Never imagine yourself not to be otherwise than . . .

. . . what it might appear to others that what you were or might have been was not otherwise than what you had been would have appeared to them to be otherwise.""

The Duchess,
Alice's Adventures in Wonderland

"Always speak the truth—
think before you speak—and
write it down afterwards."

The Red Queen,
Through the Looking-Glass

"Curtsey while you're thinking what to say, it saves time.**"**

The Red Queen,
Through the Looking-Glass

"**S**peak in French when you can't think of the English for a thing—turn out your toes as you walk—and remember who you are!"

The Red Queen,
Through the Looking-Glass

The Queen had only one way of settling all difficulties, great or small. "Off with his head!" she said, without even looking round.

The Red Queen,
Alice's Adventures in Wonderland

"No, no!" said the Queen. "Sentence first—verdict afterwards."

The Red Queen,
Alice's Adventures in Wonderland

"I can't believe that!"
said Alice.

"Can't you?" the Queen
said in a pitying tone. "Try
again: draw a long breath,
and shut your eyes."

Alice and the Red Queen,
Through the Looking-Glass

"**W**ell, in *our* country," said Alice, still panting a little, "you'd generally get to somewhere else—if you ran very fast for a long time, as we've been doing."

"A slow sort of country!"
said the Queen, "Now, here,
you see, it takes all the running
you can do, to keep in the
same place. If you want to get
somewhere else, you must run at
least twice as fast as that!"

Alice and the Red Queen,
Through the Looking-Glass

"That's the effect of living backwards," the Queen said kindly: "it always makes one a little giddy at first—"

"Living backwards!" Alice repeated in great astonishment. "I never heard of such a thing!"

"—but there's one great advantage in it, that one's memory works both ways."

"I'm sure mine only works one way," Alice remarked. "I can't remember things before they happen."

"It's a poor sort of memory that only works backwards," the Queen remarked.

The White Queen,
Through the Looking-Glass

The White Queen

Alice laughed. "There's no use trying," she said: "one can't believe impossible things."

"I daresay you haven't had much practice," said the Queen. "When I was your age, I always did it for half-an-hour a day. Why, sometimes I've believed as many as six impossible things before breakfast…"

Alice and the White Queen,
Through the Looking-Glass

She generally gave herself very good advice (though she very seldom followed it).

Alice's Adventures in Wonderland

"Give your evidence," said the King; "and don't be nervous, or I'll have you executed on the spot."

The King,
Alice's Adventures in Wonderland

It was all very well to say "Drink me," but the wise little Alice was not going to do that in a hurry.

Alice's Adventures in Wonderland

"Drink Me"

"**D**on't grunt," said Alice:
"that's not at all a proper way of
expressing yourself."

Alice,
Alice's Adventures in Wonderland

"It's always tea-time."

The Hatter,
Alice's Adventures in Wonderland

CHAPTER
FOUR

SENSE & NONESENSE

There is no denying it: there is a peculiar, wonderful sort of sense even to the nonsense that is spoken in the world that Alice discovers down the rabbit hole and through the looking-glass.

One only needs to have an open mind and a listening ear...

The Red Queen shook her head, "You may call it 'nonsense' if you like," she said, "but I've heard nonsense, compared with which that would be as sensible as a dictionary!"

The Red Queen,
Through the Looking-Glass

The Red Queen

"Off With Her Head"

The Queen turned crimson with fury, and, after glaring at her for a moment like a wild beast, began screaming "Off with her head! Off with—"

"Nonsense!" said Alice, very loudly and decidedly, and the Queen was silent.

Alice and the Red Queen,
Alice's Adventures in Wonderland

"Speak when you're spoken to!" The Queen sharply interrupted her.

"But if everybody obeyed that rule," said Alice, who was always ready for a little argument, "and if . . .

. . . you only spoke when you were spoken to, and the other person always waited for you to begin, you see nobody would ever say anything, so that—"

"Ridiculous!" cried the Queen.

Alice and the Red Queen,
Through the Looking-Glass

"It's very good jam," said the Queen.

"Well, I don't want any to-day, at any rate."

"You couldn't have it if you did want it," the Queen said. "The rule is, jam tomorrow and jam yesterday—but never jam to-day."

"It must come sometimes to 'jam to-day'," Alice objected.

"No, it can't," said the Queen. "It's jam every other day; to-day isn't any other day, you know."

"I don't understand you," said Alice. "It's dreadfully confusing."

Alice and the White Queen,
Through the Looking-Glass

The Leg of Mutton

"You look a little shy; let me introduce you to that leg of mutton," said the Red Queen. "Alice—Mutton; Mutton—Alice." The leg of mutton got up in the dish and made a little bow to Alice; and Alice returned the bow, not knowing whether to be frightened or amused.

The Red Queen,
Through the Looking-Glass

"What is an un-birthday present?"

"A present given when it isn't your birthday, of course."

Alice considered a little. "I like birthday presents best," she said at last.

"You don't know what you're talking about," cried Humpty Dumpty. "How many days are there in a year?"

"Three hundred and sixty-five," said Alice.

"And how many birthdays have you?"

"One." . . .

. . . *continued overpage*

... "And if you take one from three hundred and sixty-five, what remains?"

"Three hundred and sixty-four, of course."

Humpty Dumpty looked doubtful. "I'd rather see that done on paper," he said.

Alice and Humpty Dumpty,
Through the Looking-Glass

"What dreadful nonsense we are talking!"

Alice,
Through the Looking-Glass

"You know you say things are 'much of a muchness'—did you ever see such a thing as a drawing of a muchness?"

The Dormouse,
Alice's Adventures in Wonderland

"I want a clean cup," interrupted the Hatter: "let's all move one place on."

The Hatter,
Alice's Adventures in Wonderland

"In our country," she remarked, "there's only one day at a time."

The Red Queen said, "That's a poor thin way of doing things . . .

. . . Now here, we mostly have days and nights two or three at a time, and sometimes in the winter we take as many as five nights together—for warmth, you know."

Alice and the Red Queen,
Through the Looking-Glass

"We must have a bit of a fight, but I don't care about going on long," said Tweedledum. "What's the time now?"

Tweedledee looked at his watch, and said, "Half-past four."

"Let's fight till six, and then have dinner," said Tweedledum.

Tweedledum and Tweedledee,
Through the Looking-Glass

Tweedledee and Tweedledum

The Hatter was the first to break the silence. "What day of the month is it?" he said, turning to Alice: he had taken his watch out of his pocket, and was looking at it uneasily, shaking it every now and then, and holding it to his ear.

Alice considered a little, and then said, "The fourth."

"Two days wrong!" sighed the Hatter. "I told you butter wouldn't suit the works!" he added, looking angrily at the March Hare.

Alice and the Hatter,
Alice's Adventures in Wonderland

The executioner's argument was, that you couldn't cut off a head unless there was a body to cut it off from: that he had never had to do such a thing before, and he wasn't going to begin at his time of life.

The King's argument was, that anything that had a head could be beheaded, and that you weren't to talk nonsense.

The Queen's argument was,
that if something wasn't done
about it in less than no time,
she'd have everybody executed,
all round.

Alice's Adventures in Wonderland

"There's no sort of use in knocking," said the Footman, "and that for two reasons. First, because I'm on the same side of the door as you are; secondly, because they're making such a noise inside, no one could possibly hear you."

The Footman,
Alice's Adventures in Wonderland

"No, no! The adventures first," said the Gryphon in an impatient tone: "explanations take such a dreadful time."

The Gryphon,
Alice's Adventures in Wonderland

"I can't help it," said Alice very meekly: "I'm growing."

"You've no right to grow here," said the Dormouse.

"Don't talk nonsense," said Alice more boldly: "you know you're growing too."

"Yes, but I grow at a reasonable pace," said the Dormouse: "not in that ridiculous fashion."

Alice and the Dormouse,
Alice's Adventures in Wonderland

CHAPTER
FIVE

WHIMSICAL WORDPLAY & LESSONS ON LANGUAGE

The power of words and their
multiplicitous meanings
have a special place in the hearts
of many of the indigenous
inhabitants of Wonderland –
spar with them on the logic of
their loquacious lexicon at your
protracted peril…

"Speak English!" said the Eaglet. "I don't know the meaning of half those long words, and, what's more, I don't believe you do either!"

The Eaglet,
Alice's Adventures in Wonderland

"**B**etter say nothing at all. Language is worth a thousand pounds a word!"

The Chorus of Voices,
Through the Looking-Glass

"The master was an old Turtle—we used to call him Tortoise—"

"Why did you call him Tortoise, if he wasn't one?" Alice asked.

"We called him Tortoise because he taught us," said the Mock Turtle angrily; "really you are very dull!"

Alice and the Mock Turtle,
Alice's Adventures in Wonderland

"And how many hours a day did you do lessons?" said Alice, in a hurry to change the subject.

"Ten hours the first day," said the Mock Turtle: "nine the next, and so on."

"What a curious plan!" exclaimed Alice . . .

. . . continued overpage

The Mock Turtle

"That's the reason they're called lessons," the Gryphon remarked: "because they lessen from day to day."

Alice, the Mock Turtle and the Gryphon,
Alice's Adventures in Wonderland

"They've a temper, some of them—particularly verbs, they're the proudest—adjectives you can do anything with, but not verbs—however, I can manage the whole lot of them!"

Humpty Dumpty,
Through the Looking-Glass

"I beg your pardon?" Alice said with a puzzled air.

"I'm not offended," said Humpty Dumpty.

Alice and Humpty Dumpty,
Through the Looking-Glass

"When I use a word," Humpty Dumpty said in rather a scornful tone, "it means just what I choose it to mean—neither more nor less."

"The question is," said Alice, "whether you can make words mean so many different things."

Alice and Humpty Dumpty,
Through the Looking-Glass

"My name is Alice, but—"

"It's a stupid enough name!" Humpty Dumpty interrupted impatiently.

"What does it mean?"

"Must a name mean something?" Alice asked doubtfully.

"Of course it must," Humpty Dumpty said with a short laugh: "my name means the shape I am—and a good handsome shape it is, too. With a name like yours, you might be any shape, almost."

Alice and Humpty Dumpty,
Through the Looking-Glass

"What's the use of their having names," the Gnat said, "if they won't answer to them?"

"No use to them," said Alice; "but it's useful to the people who name them, I suppose. If not, why do things have names at all?"

Alice and the Gnat,
Through the Looking-Glass

The Gnat

"You see the earth takes twenty-four hours to turn round on its axis—"

"Talking of axes," said the Duchess, "chop off her head!"

Alice and the Duchess,
Alice's Adventures in Wonderland

"Mine is a long and sad tale!" said the Mouse, turning to Alice and sighing.

"It is a long tail, certainly," said Alice, looking down with wonder at the Mouse's tail; "but why do you call it sad?"

Alice and the Mouse,
Alice's Adventures in Wonderland

The Mouse

"Sit down, both of you, and don't speak a word till I've finished."

So they sat down, and nobody spoke for some minutes. Alice thought to herself, "I don't see how he can ever finish, if he doesn't begin."

Alice and the Mock Turtle,
Alice's Adventures in Wonderland

> "If you can see whether I'm singing or not, you've sharper eyes than most."

Humpty Dumpty,
Through the Looking-Glass

"I never heard of 'Uglification'," Alice ventured to say. "What is it?"

The Gryphon lifted up both its paws in surprise.

"Never heard of uglifying!" it exclaimed.

"You know what to beautify is, I suppose?"

. . . continued overpage

The Gryphon

"Yes," said Alice, doubtfully: "it means—to—make—anything—prettier."

"Well then," the Gryphon went on, "if you don't know what to uglify is, you are a simpleton."

Alice and the Gryphon,
Alice's Adventures in Wonderland

"That's a great deal to make one word mean," Alice said in a thoughtful tone.

"When I make a word do a lot of work like that," said Humpty Dumpty, "I always pay it extra."

Alice and Humpty Dumpty,
Through the Looking-Glass

"No wise fish would go anywhere without a porpoise."

"Wouldn't it really?" said Alice in a tone of great surprise.

"Of course not," said the Mock Turtle: "why, if a fish came to me, and told me he was going a journey, I should say 'With what porpoise?'"...

... *continued overpage*

The Mock Turtle and Gryphon

. . . "Don't you mean 'purpose'?" said Alice.

"I mean what I say," the Mock Turtle replied in an offended tone.

Alice and the Mock Turtle,
Alice's Adventures in Wonderland

"**W**ell, 'slithy' means 'lithe and slimy'. 'Lithe' is the same as 'active'. You see it's like a portmanteau—there are two meanings packed up into one word."

Humpty Dumpty,
Through the Looking-Glass

"I hadn't but just begun my tea—not above a week or so—and what with the bread-and-butter getting so thin—and the twinkling of the tea—"

"The twinkling of what?" said the King.

"It began with the tea," the Hatter replied.

"Of course twinkling begins with a T!" said the King sharply. "Do you take me for a dunce? Go on!"

The Hatter and the King,
Alice's Adventures in Wonderland

"I beg your pardon," said Alice very humbly: "you had got to the fifth bend, I think?"

"I had not!" cried the Mouse, sharply and very angrily.

"A knot!" said Alice, always ready to make herself useful, and looking anxiously about her. "Oh, do let me help to undo it!"

Alice and the Mouse,
Alice's Adventures in Wonderland

CHAPTER

SIX

CURIOUSER & CURIOUSER

—⁂—

In a world where rabbits wear waistcoats and flamingos are croquet mallets, where getting bigger and smaller is a common occurrence and being beheaded by a despotic playing card is a daily concern, "curious" only just scratches the surface…

"Curiouser and curiouser!" cried Alice (she was so much surprised, that for the moment she quite forgot how to speak good English).

Alice,
Alice's Adventures in Wonderland

"Well! I've often seen a cat without a grin," thought Alice; "but a grin without a cat! It's the most curious thing I ever saw in all my life!"

Alice,
Alice's Adventures in Wonderland

Alice thought she had never seen such a curious croquet-ground in all her life: it was all ridges and furrows; the croquet-balls were live hedgehogs, the mallets live flamingos, and the soldiers had to double themselves up and to stand upon their hands and feet, to make the arches.

Alice's Adventures in Wonderland

Croquet

"When I used to read fairy-tales, I fancied that kind of thing never happened, and now here I am in the middle of one! There ought to be a book written about me, that there ought!"

Alice,
Alice's Adventures in Wonderland

"The Duchess! The Duchess!
Oh my dear paws! Oh my fur
and whiskers! She'll get me
executed, as sure as ferrets are
ferrets!"

The White Rabbit,
Alice's Adventures in Wonderland

Alice

"Who cares for you?"
said Alice, (she had grown to her
full size by this time.) "You're
nothing but a pack of cards!"

Alice,
Alice's Adventures in Wonderland

She hastily put down the bottle, saying to herself, "That's quite enough—I hope I sha'n't grow any more—As it is, I can't get out at the door—I do wish I hadn't drunk quite so much!"

Alice,
Alice's Adventures in Wonderland

"If it had grown up," she said to herself, "it would have made a dreadfully ugly child: but it makes rather a handsome pig, I think."

Alice,
Alice's Adventures in Wonderland

"*The* Queen of Hearts, she made some tarts,

All on a summer day:

The Knave of Hearts, he stole those tarts,

And took them quite away!"

The White Rabbit,
Alice's Adventures in Wonderland

The White Rabbit

"Oh dear! Oh dear! I shall be too late!"

The White Rabbit,
Alice's Adventures in Wonderland

H

ow she longed to get out of that dark hall, and wander about among those beds of bright flowers and those cool fountains, but she could not even get her head though the doorway; "and even if my head would go through," thought poor Alice, "it would be of very little use without my shoulders."

Alice's Adventures in Wonderland

"I wish I hadn't cried so much!" said Alice, as she swam about, trying to find her way out. "I shall be punished for it now, I suppose, by being drowned in my own tears! That will be a queer thing, to be sure! However, everything is queer to-day."

Alice,
Alice's Adventures in Wonderland

Drowning in Tears

—⁓—

"Twas brillig, and the slithy toves

　　Did gyre and gimble in the wabe;

　　All mimsy were the borogoves,

　　And the mome raths outgrabe.

　　'Beware the Jabberwock, my son!

The jaws that bite, the claws that catch!

Beware the Jubjub bird, and shun

The frumious Bandersnatch!'

'Jabberwocky',
Through the Looking-Glass

"I'm Late!"